Dear Parent:
Your child's love of reading starts here.

Every child learns to read in a different way and at his or her own speed. Some go back and forth between reading levels and read favorite books again and again. Others read through each level in order. You can help your young reader improve and become more confident by encouraging his or her own interests and abilities. From books your child reads with you to the first books he or she reads alone, there are I Can Read Books for every stage of reading:

SHARED READING
Basic language, word repetition, and whimsical illustrations, ideal for sharing with your emergent reader

BEGINNING READING
Short sentences, familiar words, and simple concepts for children eager to read on their own

READING WITH HELP
Engaging stories, longer sentences, and language play for developing readers

READING ALONE
Complex plots, challenging vocabulary, and high-interest topics for the independent reader

ADVANCED READING
Short paragraphs, chapters, and exciting themes for the perfect bridge to chapter books

I Can Read Books have introduced children to the joy of reading since 1957. Featuring award-winning authors and illustrators and a fabulous cast of beloved characters, I Can Read Books set the standard for beginning readers.

A lifetime of discovery begins with the magical words "I Can Read!"

Visit www.icanread.com for information
on enriching your child's reading experience.

bag

 pie

 book

 ponies

 butterflies

 rainbow

 butterfly

 scooter

 clouds

 sugar

 clover

 sun

 cupboard

 sunflowers

 grass

 wind

Very Lucky Ponies

by Ruth Benjamin
illustrated by Lyn Fletcher

HarperCollins*Publishers*

It was a rainy day.

The were dark.

Serendipity saw

something in the .

It was shiny and green.

It was a four-leaf .

She picked up the .

Suddenly the rain stopped.

The ☀ came out.

The dark ☁ went away.

A 🌈 sparkled

in the sky.

"Wow!" said Serendipity.

"I think this

is a lucky 🍀."

At home, Serendipity

found her missing .

"I have looked all over

for this !" she said.

"This really is lucky."

Serendipity wanted

to share the 🍀

with the 🐴 .

She gave the 🍀

to Desert Rose.

"Now you will have

good luck, too," she said.

"Thank you," said Desert Rose

"I will bring the 🍀

when I go to pick flowers."

Desert Rose found a field

filled with pretty  .

She had never seen

 before.

"This really is lucky,"

she said.

Then she gave the

to Scootaloo.

Scootaloo rode her

to look for  .

She saw a

with a  pattern.

She had never seen

a before!

"This really is lucky,"

she said.

Cupcake was baking a .

Oh, no! She ran out of .

Scootaloo came by and gave

the to Cupcake.

Cupcake checked the .

She saw a big of .

"This really is lucky,"

she said.

Cupcake wished

all the

could have a lucky .

Just as she made her wish,

a big gust of came.

The blew away.

"Oh, no!" called the .

Our lucky 🍀 is gone!"

The 🐴 looked all over

for the 🍀.

But they did not find it.

"We should not be sad,"

Desert Rose told the  .

"We do not need the

to feel lucky.

We are lucky that

we have each other.

We are good friends!"

"Yes, we are!"

said the  .

"We are very lucky !"

Then they shared a

under a !